S0-AER-729

WAYNE PUBLIC LIBRARY

AUG 3 1 2010

# My Big Fat Secret

## How Jenna Takes Control of Her Emotions and Eating

by Lynn R. Schechter, PhD
illustrated by Jason Chin

Magination Press
Washington, DC
American Psychological Association

Vacation Photos

Jenna's Email

https://www.mybigfatsecret.com/copyright_page.html

To my beloved children Leah and Leo, for their love which feeds and empowers me— LRS

For my father— JC

Copyright © 2010 by Magination Press. All rights reserved. Except as permitted under the United States Copyright Act of 1976, no part of this publication may be reproduced or distributed in any form or by any means, or stored in a database or retrieval system, without the prior written permission of the publisher.

Published by
MAGINATION PRESS
An Educational Publishing Foundation Book
American Psychological Association
750 First Street, NE
Washington, DC 20002

For more information about our books, including a complete catalog, please write to us, call 1-800-374-2721, or visit our website at www.maginationpress.com.

Printed by Phoenix Color, Rockaway, New Jersey

Library of Congress Cataloging-in-Publication Data
Schechter, Lynn R.
My big fat secret : how Jenna takes control of her emotions and eating / by Lynn R. Schechter ; illustrated by Jason Chin.
p. cm.
"American Psychological Association."
Summary: Through email exchanges with her cousin, best friend, parents, and school counselor, twelve-year-old Jenna reveals a growing awareness of the causes of her emotional overeating and what she is doing to take control.
ISBN-13: 978-1-4338-0540-0 (hardcover : alk. paper)
ISBN-10: 1-4338-0540-5 (hardcover : alk. paper)
ISBN-13: 978-1-4338-0541-7 (pbk. : alk. paper)
ISBN-10: 1-4338-0541-3 (pbk. : alk. paper) [1. Overweight persons–Fiction. 2. Body image–Fiction. 3. Popularity–Fiction. 4. Middle schools–Fiction. 5. Schools–Fiction. 6. Email–Fiction.] I. Chin, Jason, 1978- ill. II. Title.
PZ7.S3422My 2010
[Fic]–dc22
2009008610

10 9 8 7 6 5 4 3 2 1

ww.mybigfatsecret.com/title_page.html

My Big Fat Secret

Vacation Photos

Jenna's Email

From: Lynn R. Schechter, PhD
To: Reader

Every kid just wants to fit in, to be accepted and liked by others. Nobody wants to be teased or picked on or bullied. That's the worst. If you're an overweight kid, then you know how hard it can be just to get through each day. Other kids at school and sometimes even your own family members can make you feel ugly, self-conscious, or ashamed of how you look and who you are. People might even make comments about what you eat and say things like, "You really don't need to eat that, do you?" or even worse, call you mean names.

This is Jenna's story in *My Big Fat Secret*. When you're like Jenna, you feel so hurt that you do the one thing that always seems to make you feel better—at least for a while—you EAT! This is what happens in Jenna's world. She eats to deal with her feelings, even though she realizes that it only makes her problem of being overweight even worse. She is caught in a vicious cycle of emotional eating, just like so many overweight kids are.

With the help of her friends, family, teachers, and professionals, Jenna finds healthy ways to deal with her feelings and that she can stop emotional eating. She realizes that she's not a bad person because she is overweight and that she is not alone. Jenna takes control of her emotions and eating and begins to make basic changes in her daily life which help her to become a healthier and happier girl.

If you are an overweight kid, please know that you are not alone. You can change what you do, take charge of your feelings, and get control over your eating. It won't be easy at first, that's for sure. But once you make up your mind, you can do it! You really can!

Your friend,

Dr. Schechter

From: Sara
To: Jenna
Sent: Sunday, August 30, 1:13 PM
Subject: Checking in cuz
Attachment: Funland.jpg

Hey Jenna! How's my favorite cousin? I haven't talked to you in forever, since my 15<sup>th</sup> b-day. One more year and I'm driving! Ok, I'll have a learner's permit, but whatever. How is everything?! How are guitar lessons going? I'm sure you're an even more amazing player than you were the last time you played for me. Anyway, fill me in on your entire life.

Life here is fine, not too exciting. Gabe is as annoying as ever – you know how little brothers are. I'm off, Mom's calling me. Write back…right now! And check out the pic of us from Funland! Enjoy!

XOXOXO

Sarita

Hi cuz! I'm so sorry I've been totally lame about writing :-( It's been so long and I just don't have good excuses so this is gonna be a long update :-) I think of you a lot and wonder how you're doing out there in California, with all that sun and stuff, while I'm stuck here in NY. I so wish I lived out there near you, then we could go to Funland ALL THE TIME! Thanks for sending the pic of us from my last trip! It was so awesome and fun ;-) I'll have to ask Mom and Dad to plan another trip soon!

So let's see, what's been going on over gere? (I meant here! LOL! I'm having a hard time typing b/c I still have chip stuff on my fingers!) I went to camp this summer and took guitar classes. Camp was okay but just like always I didn't fit in with the other girls. I made some friends but the really popular girls didn't like me. I don't know why…but I don't really like them either. They are so fake and so perfect…and you know I'm not that! So that was kind of hard. But I did make a couple of friends and I also really liked my counselor Sandra – she was so cool. It's a bummer that summer is totally over.

Can you believe I'm 12 now and in 7th GRADE! I used to think of the kids in 7th grade as being so much older and now I'm one of them! That's like I always think of you as being so much older since you're almost 16 (!)…I can only dream of being as cool as you are when I'm that OLD! LOL!!

Ciao for now,
J.

From: Sara
To: Jenna
Sent: Monday, August 31, 6:02 PM
Subject: RE: RE: Checking in cuz

Very funny cuz! Sixteen is cool though. I'll send you an invite to my sweet 16. Keep your fingers crossed and maybe your parents will fly you out here to celebrate with me!!

Sorry to hear that some of the girls weren't that nice at camp. I went through that. Middle school girls can be so mean. Sounds like you handled it well though. Trust me, high school is better!

Adios,
Sarita

From: Jenna
To: Sara
Sent: Monday, August 31, 6:19 PM
Subject: RE: RE: RE: Checking in cuz

I was really nervous about going to middle school, but so far it seems pretty okay. Thank goodness at least I have my best friend Chris. I think you met him last time you were out here, the guy with the cute smile ;-) We go to different schools but he's in my guitar classes. It's really awesome having someone like him here who likes the same things as I do, like music and animals. I know you like that stuff too, but you're so far away :-( We both like to practice playing our guitars a lot. Chris is always there no matter what is going on in my life, and I was just realizing that we've known each other for 7 years – since kindergarten! I wish we went to the same middle school so we could see each other every day.

But my main problem still has not gone away. And you of all people know what that problem is…my weight and how big I am compared to the other girls. It's been really hard. I just feel so down sometimes and like everyone's always looking at me and thinking how gross I look. I hate it. I REALLY, REALLY hate it!!!!! And I HATE how I look too. I hate looking in the mirror.

6th grade was just so tough – kids at school were so mean to me. Especially in gym. These girls Allyson and Madison were the worst! Calling me names like Miss Piggy and Jenna the Hut. I really hope middle school is better. Bigger school, more people – maybe I can just kind of disappear. I'm trying to look forward to it, but I have a feeling things won't be that different…I hope they will be. I hope!

From: Sara
To: Jenna
Sent: Monday, August 31, 6:36 PM
Subject: RE: RE: RE: RE: Checking in Cuz

Things will get better, Jenna. I can feel it! And I know you think you're kind of big, and maybe you can lose *some* weight, but you're not HUGE! You remind me of my friend Marybelle who was also a little bit big. She did different things so she could feel better. Like, she started to exercise more and to eat different things – healthy stuff, like fruits and vegetables, instead of junk. Just something to think about Jen!

From: Chris
To: Jenna
Sent: Monday, September 7, 8:07 PM
Subject: howdy

Sup Jen? I meant to tell you that you looked cool today. You're a real rocker chick, for sure.

I'm psyched for practice tomorrow…I've been really working on this one song for a while and it finally sounds pretty awesome.
How R U?
Chris

From: Jenna
To: Chris
Sent: Monday, September 7, 8:40 PM
Subject: RE: howdy

Hey dude. Good to hear from ya. I'm doing fine. Thanks about the outfit. I was so glad the store actually had that jacket in my SIZE!

Can't wait to hear you play tomorrow. I better start getting ready for bed.

Good night! - J.

From: Chris
To: Jenna
Sent: Monday, September 7, 8:58 PM
Subject: RE: RE: howdy
Attachment: Jamming.jpg

You and your SIZE! So maybe you can lose a few pounds. But you think you're HUGE and YOU'RE NOT!!
Anyway, before you sleep, check out this cool photo of you and me jamming last week at practice.
Later.

Jen,

I felt kind of sad when I read your last email because you are such an awesome, smart, and beautiful girl and I hate to hear that you get down so much on yourself about how you look. I know we talked about your weight problem when you were here (I was so PROUD of you for opening up to me because I know that wasn't easy for you to do). I know how those skinny popular girls (or who I like to call the "perfect" girls!!) are...they just ignore you or, even worse, give you dirty looks or comments which hurt so bad. I wish I was out there near you so I could give them a piece of my MIND!!! But not too much of it – I still need it at least until I finish college!! LOL ;-)

I know that it's hard for you to not pay attention to them when they bother you about your weight, but I really want you to try to ignore them. You have so much to offer and are SO COOL!! They've got NOTHING on you!! I'm always here for you whenever you need someone to listen or give you advice – and I also wish we lived closer.

XOXO
Sarita

You are so sweet Sara. You always make me feel better. I'm going to try to focus on the positive stuff in my life like my family, my friends (especially Chris), and my guitar playing. I just hope things get better at school. I'm out!

XOXOX,
J.

Jen, like I've always said, I'm ALWAYS here for you. You are my most favorite cuz in the WORLD!!! :-) We always have a blast whenever we are together and I just want you to know that I NEVER think of you as fat or big or whatever. I only think of you as a cool, fun person to hang with. You can rock that guitar! And I would just kill for your hair!! :-) j/k – I wouldn't really kill ya!! LOL!! By the way, check out this picture of you with your 'rents from your last visit…you all look so cute!

But seriously, I want you to remember how you always told me how much better you feel after you tell me about what's on your mind and what's going on in your life. Like I told you before: DON'T HOLD YOUR FEELINGS IN SO MUCH!!! Email me more often instead of every couple of months. I LOVE getting email! And do you remember how I told you about that time like a couple of years ago when I had gotten really down in the dumps and my parents sent me to talk to that counselor? I was kind of nervous and thought it was dumb, but it actually really helped me when I had a place to get stuff off my chest. So I'm not saying you need a counselor (or maybe you do? – something to think about!) but at least for now you always have ME!!!

Love ya.
XOXO,
Sarita

From: Mom and Dad
To: Jenna
Sent: Thursday, September 10, 9:18 AM
Subject: Party

Hi, Jenna. We just wanted to remind you about the block party that will be in Nana's neighborhood this coming Sunday afternoon. We'll leave a little bit early – around 11:30 AM – so that we can pick up a cake from the bakery. I already bought chips, candy, and soda. Don't forget!

Love,
Mom

From: Jenna
To: Mom and Dad
Sent: Thursday, September 10, 12:14 PM
Subject: RE: Party

Ok Mom, no problem. I'll make sure I have my homework done before we leave. Bye.

From: Jenna
To: Chris
Sent: Saturday, September 12, 8:42 PM
Subject: I feel so bad

Chris,

I can't believe what I just did. I'm so embarrassed right now but I need to tell somebody, and I guess you're it. My mom had bought all this candy and chips for the block party tomorrow, and I just ate a whole bunch of it. I hid the wrappers. My mom is going to be so mad when she realizes we have to go shopping again in the morning before the party. I'm so lame and I feel so bad (and sick) right now.

J.

From: Chris
To: Jenna
Sent: Saturday, September 12, 9:50 PM
Subject: RE: I feel so bad
Attachment: KidsWhoEatTooMuch.pdf

I found this article on the internet about kids who eat even when they're not hungry like you do. It seems like there are a lot of kids who do that. That's why there are so many big kids around these days I guess. Read it, I hope it helps!

# Kids Who Eat Too Much:
## Tips for How You Can Stop Overeating

by Lynn R. Schechter, PhD, child psychologist

Lots of kids overeat. If you eat when you're not hungry, you might be eating because you're bored or angry or lonely or because it's a habit. But you can do something about it! Here are some basic tips for kids on ways that you can stop overeating and break this unhealthy habit:

**Listen to your body.** Pay attention to when your stomach is actually hungry. If you're not actually hungry in your stomach when you eat, then you're overeating.

**Chew your food slowly.** Pay attention to how much you eat at meals.

**Put your fork down.** When you're eating, put your fork or spoon down in between bites and really enjoy your food. Don't just shove it in your mouth!

**Drink a lot of water.** Sometimes you may eat when you're really just thirsty!

**Pick healthy foods.** When you eat, make sure you make healthy choices like vegetables and fruits, since these are good for you and they fill you up, too.

**Think before you eat.** Don't grab a whole bag of chips or other junk food when you're doing something mindless like watching TV. You're not paying attention to how much you're eating and the next thing you know, the whole bag is empty!

**Don't eat when you're bored.** Plan ahead to figure out what you can do instead of eating. Call a friend, go for a walk, read a book, work on a painting. Anything you like to do!

**Keep a food journal.** Use it to write down what you eat each day, even if it's just for a week. Write down everything you eat and then take a look at it. Make sure you don't cheat! When you review your entries ask yourself: are you eating extra food when you don't need it, when you're not even hungry? If the answer is yes, then you need to figure out other activities you can do instead of eating!

These are just some basic tips that can help kids stop overeating. Give them a try (and come up with your own) and see how they can help you!

From: Jenna
To: Chris
Sent: Saturday, September 12, 9:20 PM
Subject: RE: RE: I feel so bad

Thanks so much for the article. It's good to know I'm not the only one!

C U Monday!

J.

From: Jenna
To: Sara
Sent: Monday, September 14, 2:33 PM
Subject: Can't believe it!!!

Sara, you're not EVEN going to BELIEVE THIS!!!!!!!! I am SO ANGRY right now!!!! I'm serious, you won't even believe this when I tell you…

Ok, so yesterday, Mom and Dad and I, we all went to a block party in Nana's neighborhood…afterwards, Nana told Mom and Dad that she thought I had PACKED ON A LOT OF POUNDS (!!!!!!!!!) and that I needed to see a doctor to make sure **NOTHING'S WRONG WITH ME!!!!!!!!!! Can you believe that?!** It was just SO BRUTAL!!!! And to top it all off, **MOM AND DAD AGREED WITH HER!**

So, I'm fat and I might have something terribly wrong with me. LIFE TOTALLY STINKS RIGHT NOW!!!

I miss you and soooo wish you were here :-(

Oh my gosh, Jen! That sucks!!! I'm so upset for you right now I almost don't know what to write. I also can't believe Nana would say something just so downright mean like that…I mean, first of all, even if she thought that you were overweight, she could say it in a nicer way or in a different way…but to say that you'd packed on a lot of pounds! Who says that?!!! URGH!!! :-(

I've been thinking a lot about this. Remember my friend Marybelle I told you about? She's a little big like you. I know that she went to her doctor and she was really a big help to her…she gave her really good advice about how to eat better stuff and she also checked out to make sure that she was healthy…I know how you told me you really don't like going to the doctor because you hate to get on the scale (and I know I can't even blame you for that…I know a lot of skinny girls who hate to get weighed too! And even some of them think they're too big! YIKES!! But that is a whole other serious problem…). So I guess what I'm saying is that even though what Nana and your parents said was really not in the best way – it was actually just plain mean – maybe your doctor could be a help to you if you give him a chance…

Think about it. And I'm so sorry for how sad you must've felt… Sending you positive vibes, always!!

XOXOX,
Sarita

From: Jenna
To: Sara
Sent: Monday, September 14, 3:39 PM
Subject: RE: RE: Can't believe it!!!

I don't know if I'm ready to go to a doctor. Why is everyone just always so focused on my size? It really hurts me so much. I still can't believe what they said… I feel like such a defect. Like I'm just one BIG walking, talking DEFECT. It's like people just say, okay, we love you Jenna, you're so cool, we love you just as you are, NOW GO AHEAD AND CHANGE!! It really makes me mad!! And sad too.

I know what you're saying about the doctor being a help to your friend…I don't know. I'm just so scared of what he's going to say. And I just HATE getting on the scale and seeing for real just how big I am. It's like I can almost pretend that I'm not fat if I can just not look at that number. I HATE THIS!!

Well, I'll let you know what happens. I think my mom and dad are going to make an appointment for me in a few weeks. Thanks for all your words of wisdom.

Hugs,
J.

From: Mom and Dad
To: Jenna
Sent: Monday, September 14, 4:03 PM
Subject: Doctor's appointment

Jenna, I had the feeling you might not want to start talking about this in person, so I thought I'd send you an email and then you, Dad, and I can talk about it after dinner tonight. We know how upset you were about what happened with Nana the other night.

We have to admit that she certainly didn't pick her words very well, and we probably made a mistake in telling you exactly what she said and how she said it. It wasn't nice and we're sorry if it upset you.

Dad and I love you so much, and we know from what you've told us that you definitely are concerned about your weight and your eating habits. Maybe we haven't done enough to help you. I know that I haven't helped by doing things like pretending I didn't notice that you ate so much of the candy and chips that I had bought for the block party. I didn't know what to say to you. I think it might not be a bad idea to have a visit with the doctor to get some advice and just to make sure you're ok. We don't want you to worry and we think that probably everything IS OK!! But it never hurts to get a professional's opinion, too...after all, that's why they went to school for so many years, right?

We'll talk about this more tonight, and I'll let you know when I make the appointment.

Love,
Mom (and Dad)

| From: Jenna<br>To: Mom and Dad<br>Sent: Monday, September 14, 4:13 PM<br>Subject: RE: Doctor's appointment |  |
| --- | --- |

OK Mom. Yeah, let me know when you make the appointment so I know to practice taking deep breaths so I'm not so nervous. And yep, it really did hurt my feelings the way that Nana and you guys mentioned my size. It hurt me A LOT. Honestly, I was and am still pretty upset and angry with you guys. I just don't understand why everyone focuses so much on my weight and how I look. It really hurts me.

And yeah, I did eat some of the candy and chips you bought from the party, I admit it. I just don't get why you pretended not to notice.

From: Mom and Dad
To: Jenna
Sent: Monday, September 14, 4:44 PM
Subject: RE: RE: Doctor's appointment

Jenna, I know this is hard. I apologize for not being more honest with you about noticing the missing candy. I think you're right. Not saying something isn't helping you. Your dad and I have been sending you some confusing messages. We have felt uncomfortable bringing up the subject with you, and it wasn't until the party that we realized maybe we should be more direct with you and also consider the visit to Dr. Hy. We love you and you are always beautiful to us no matter what.

Love,
Mom

From: Jenna
To: Mom and Dad
Sent: Monday, September 14, 5:03 PM
Subject: RE: RE: RE: Doctor's appointment

I love you guys so much too, and if you think maybe it would help me to get Dr. Hy's advice, then I'm up for it. I have to admit, I don't know what to do and I need someone else to help me. I guess I do need to talk to you and dad tonight. Thanks for saying that it's not good for you and dad to send me mixed messages. See you later when I get home from guitar practice. Luv ya.

Hi Chris,

I hope you are having a great day because I just had the worst day today at school. EVER. You know how they all make fun of me? Well today was the worst yet. That girl Madison wrote a note about me and passed it around to EVERYONE in class. I looked over Allyson's shoulder and guess what the note said? It said, "Jenna's a big fat PIG!" They had even drawn a picture of a pig and named it Jenna! That hurt my feelings so much I thought I was going to throw up! I asked Ms. Richardson if I could go to the bathroom. I went there and just cried and cried and cried. Did you hear me all the way across town? :-( :-( :-(

I felt so disgusting and lonely. I really hate Madison and Allyson! Urrrgg! Why are they always so mean to me? Can't they just pick on someone else for a change? It's not fair! It makes me SO MAD!!

PS – I stole the note and scanned it for you so you can see it for your own eyes.

Hey Jenna – Who cares what Allyson or Madison or ANYONE else thinks about you?
You're so cool. That note is pretty mean though. WOW!!

Chris, I know you didn't mean it, but your email kind of hurt my feelings. It's SOOO easy for you to say that I shouldn't care what they think about me. First of all, you're a guy and you just don't know how mean girls can be!! You aren't BIG like me. I used to not be able to even say it, but I'm FAT. Face it. And that's my biggest problem! Do you know how hard it is being a BIG FAT PIG in a school full of skinny, pretty girls? It's almost impossible!!! And every time I have a bad day like this, I go right home for my secret food stash and pig out. (I actually do this a lot – can't you tell???) Whenever I'm upset or angry or sad I eat like 4 packs of peanut candies or three packs of chips or an entire bag of cookies or whatever I can find. It makes me feel so gross.

I just think I'm fat already, and kids make fun of me and hate me because I'm fat. So what am I supposed to do? I know that this is going to make me FATTER! I hate doing this. I know I shouldn't. I always feel gross after. But it happens every time. I can't seem to stop!

But you know what? When I'm eating I forget about all my anger and sad feelings. It's like sometimes I just feel like food is my

SECRET BEST FRIEND (no offense, Chris). It's just always there for me and it always makes me feel better when I'm angry or sad. It doesn't tell me I'm FAT and it never, ever calls me names. I can't help it. It's just so hard to stop doing this. I wish that I could stop doing it….but when I feel so sad or so angry, I don't even know what else to do!!

From: Chris
To: Jenna
Sent: Wednesday, September 16, 7:10 PM
Subject: RE: RE: RE: WORST DAY OF MY LIFE!!!

Save some candy for me! j/k ;-) And I'm sorry – I know I can't totally understand what you're going through. But remember, I do hear a lot of stuff about how girls are from my sister, and yeah, it does sound like you girls can be pretty harsh on each other!! And I thought the DUDES were bad!!!

Listen, Jenna, I think you're awesome. Remember you told me that even though the guitar strings kind of hurt your fingers and sometimes you felt weird doing performances, you love playing guitar? You said that you could just focus on playing and forget about all your problems? How cool is that?! You totally could have told me how you felt…. And just like our parents always say – OPEN UP.

You know you'll probably get another blue ribbon at the science fair this year, and Mademoiselle Narby is totally going to pick you to recite from Le Petit Prince at your school's French night. You'll probably be elected president of the French Club too! Your accent is très French.

Try to forget about the BFP Incident. LOL.

p.s. You are an excellent guitar player too.
p.p.s. Allyson and Madison don't even know how to play guitar!!!

Jenna,

I just wanted you to know that we spoke to Dr. Hy. I made an appointment for you at the end of this month, on September 28th at 9 AM to see him. Both Dad and I can go with you if you like, or if you prefer to go with just one of us then just let me know.

We love you and are always here for you! We know that this isn't going to be easy, but we're ready to do anything to help you. Remember how Dad told you about when he was young he wanted to try out for the football team but since he wasn't so big like the other boys he didn't think he could make it? But then he put in a lot of hard work building up his muscles and getting stronger and then he made it! It just goes to show you that we believe that you can accomplish a hard change in your life if you put in the hard work needed to make it come true! And we'll always be there for you as your own personal cheerleaders! (That is, if you don't mind our silly costumes – wink wink!)

Love,

Mom (and Dad)

GULP!! Ok Mom. I'll put it on my calendar. I think I want both you and Dad to go with me. Love you too. And thanks for reminding me about that story of how Dad made the football team even though he wasn't so humongous like the other boys. It's kind of funny…he wanted to get bigger and I want to get smaller!! LOL!!

By the way, I'm going to be staying long at guitar practice with Chris after school today, so can you keep my dinner for me? Thanks.

See ya lata alligatas!

From: Jenna
To: Chris
Sent: Thursday, September 17, 12:15 PM
Subject: YIKES!!

Hey dude! Looking fwd to seeing you at practice today. Just wanted you to know that my mom just emailed me…they (she and my dad) made the appointment for me to see the doc. I'm so scared, but I'm going to have to suck it up like you said the other day. Maybe he will be able to help…

C U - J.

From: Chris
To: Jenna
Sent: Thursday, September 17, 1:27 PM
Subject: RE: YIKES!!
Attachment: NEWGIRLSGYM.pdf

Oh man…..that is going to be tough for ya, I know. But I'm proud of you Jen because at least you're keeping an open mind that maybe the doc can give you some good advice so you won't have to stress out so much. I respect you for that A LOT!!! And I also respect that you're so committed to learning how to be a better musician…guitar is one of the hardest instruments to learn!!

Looking fwd to practice too…I've been learning some new tunes which I'll have to share w/ya…

C U 2 – C.

p.s. U RULE!! Also, I found this flyer about a new gym for girls where you can do yoga and swimming, and the girls look like they're not just annoying skinny types! Check it out!!

From: Jenna
To: Mademoiselle Narby
Sent: Monday, September 21, 4:02 PM
Subject: Merci Beaucoup

Dear Mademoiselle Narby,

Thanks so much for listening to me after my tough time in gym class today. Gym is always rough for me, as you know since I talked to you about this before. It's bad enough that I get picked last! *Mon ami* Chris just sent me info about a new girls' gym where I can do yoga and swim after school. I think I might join.

But talking *avec vous* really did make me feel a whole lot better. I still wonder if Coach Andrews will let me wear sweat pants instead of the new shorts. Do you think he'd let me? This is really embarrassing, but my legs rub together when I'm wearing shorts and it's just not comfortable either and sometimes I get a rash which really hurts. *Merci beaucoup* again! I'm off to study for le French quiz!

*Au revoir,*

Jeannette

From: Mademoiselle Narby
To: Jenna
Sent: Monday, September 21, 5:51 PM
Subject: RE: Merci Beaucoup
Attachment: FrenchClub.jpg

*Chere* Jeannette,

I'm so glad I could be there for you today. You can always come and talk to me if you have any problems, and remember Mrs.

Gonzalez, the school counselor, is always here for you, too. As your teacher, I must ask if you've talked to your parents about everything that's going on. I'm sure they want to help! I know what you're going through. When I was your age, the other girls in class used to pick on me because I stuttered. It really helped when I talked to my friends and family about how it made me feel even though it didn't make the girls stop teasing me. And you should keep talking, too!

Like I said today, you're such a smart, sensitive, and special young lady. Just try not to let the other kids know how upset they make you feel—it just adds fuel to the fire. I know it's hard when you're a sensitive person not to let others know how hurt you are, though. I really do appreciate that you have the trust and confidence in me to share with me what you're going through.

*Au revoir,*

Mlle. Narby

PS – I thought you'd like a picture from the last French Club meeting. You look *magnifique*!

From: Jenna
To: Mademoiselle Narby
Sent: Monday, September 21, 6:09 PM
Subject: RE: RE: Merci Beaucoup

Mlle. Narby,

*Je suis* SO glad that I have you for my teacher!

Jeannette

From: Mademoiselle Narby
To: Jenna
Sent: Monday, September 21, 6:18 PM
Subject: RE: RE: RE: Merci Beaucoup

Jeannette,

I, too, am so glad I have you as my student! I just wish that you would really pay more attention to all of your terrific qualities. *Tu est fantastique!* You're a *bonne amie* to the other kids in class, you're a great student, you have a wonderful sense of humor, and you love to learn. It's been a real treat to get to know you!

In terms of the shorts, you could ask Coach Andrews if he can make an exception for you, but I don't think he'll allow it. Also, wearing the sweat pants might draw attention to you from the other girls in class, which it sounds like you don't want. Please let me know what he says if you decide to talk to him. Have a wonderful night, Jenna, and I'll see you in school tomorrow.

*A demain,*

Mademoiselle Narby

Sweet pea—

We're so proud of you for how well you handled going to the doctor this morning. And I know we're all relieved to know that Dr. Hy ruled out any medical problems or medical reasons for your being overweight!

It took a lot of courage to listen and *hear* what he had to say. When you told us you were ready to start making changes tonight, your mom and I were so proud. It's not an easy thing to accept that you have to change—believe me, I know. Remember when I quit smoking? It wasn't easy! I slipped up a bunch of times until I finally stopped completely.

We're going to support you 110% and are even going to change parts of our lifestyle that aren't very healthy, like my French fry addiction and your mom's soda habit. This will be a family change—you don't have to do this alone!

Just let us know how else we can help. We could start cooking together—your mom came up with the great idea of making a menu for the week. Anyway, these are just a few ideas. We're here to help and support you.

And number one, WE LOVE YOU!

Dad (and Mom)

Oh, Dad—

You're so cheesy. I'm between periods in the library. I'm not skipping class. Thanks for your help. You and Mom are awesome. Cooking sounds really good and it'll be fun to try new recipes. Remember when we made that soufflé together for French club? It was yummy, but I don't know how healthy it was.

Maybe tonight we could talk some more about what I can do to control my eating? Last night I finished that whole bag of chips that was in the kitchen! I knew I shouldn't have, but I did…I guess I was bored or something. :-( It does make me feel better to know that when you tried to stop smoking you messed up sometimes. It's so hard to change. I think I decided to talk to Mrs. Gonzalez, my school counselor, to get some advice. I'm kind of scared but I know that I can do it with you and Mom behind me. The bell just rang…got to go to algebra!

Lots of love to both you guys!! C U lata :-)

ME!!

PS: I found a cool gym that I might want to try out with Mom… could we talk about that tonight too?

Glad to hear you weren't playing hooky, Jenna! I'm just joking. Your mom and I are just so proud of you—I don't think you really have any idea how proud.

Mom and I would be happy to help you think of ways to get your eating under better control. Thanks for being honest about what happened last night with the chips…You will make mistakes, everyone does when they're trying to change, but the important thing is to start over again and talk about it so we can help you. I think, for one, your mom and I will just have to remember to stop bringing junk food into the house. It's too tempting and it really isn't healthy anyway to have it around. I know that I've been tempted a lot to snack on that junk food even when I'm not hungry, so I can relate. I was looking for some healthy meals we could make at home and found a couple of recipes. Check them out. We can go shopping for the ingredients together! And thanks for telling me about the girls' gym—we'll talk about it tonight. This weekend we can take a family trip to check it out.

I think the more that you keep busy with your friends and your schoolwork, play your wonderful guitar, and start doing exercise, the less you'll want to "pig out." When you start to see that you can change your eating habits and you feel and look better (although you'll ALWAYS be beautiful in our eyes) the easier it will be for you to stop eating when you're not hungry.

We also think it's great that you have decided to go to talk to Mrs. Gonzalez. Maybe she has some advice for all of us!

Love,
Dad

# MINI PIZZAS

Who doesn't love pizza? These are fun to make and you can put all sorts of tasty, healthy toppings on them too! You don't have to put every topping that's listed here, and maybe there are some others that you like better. Experiment and have fun!

This recipe makes 1 serving

## You'll need

- 1 baking sheet

## Ingredients

- 1 whole-wheat English muffin, split in half
- 1/4 cup pasta sauce
- 2 slices of mozzarella (1 per muffin half) or other grated cheese
- 1 tablespoon black olives, sliced into rings
- 3 rings of red or yellow peppers
- 1/4 cup chopped tuna in water, drained
- 1 tablespoon canned sweet corn, drained
- 4–5 baby mushrooms, sliced (optional)
- 6 chunks fresh pineapple, cut thinly (optional)

## Preparation

Before you start, makes sure you have adult supervision.

Preheat the oven to 325 degrees. Toast the sliced English muffins on both sides. Spread pasta sauce on each half. Arrange your toppings on top of the pasta sauce, with the cheese going on last. Place muffins onto a baking sheet in the oven and watch carefully. Bake until cheese is melted, about 5–7 minutes. Allow muffins to cool a little before eating.

Serve with a small salad (and low-calorie dressing!). Have fun and enjoy!

# FRUITY KEBABS

This is a super-easy dessert. There's nothing to it but yummy, juicy fruit!! You'll want to make these just before you plan to eat them, otherwise some of the fruits will turn brown.

The number of servings you can make depends upon how many fruits you use.

## You'll need

- 6–8 wooden skewers (depending upon how many you want to make)

## Ingredients

- Fresh pineapple
- Bananas
- Fresh melon (cantaloupe, watermelon, honeydew)
- Apples
- Kiwis
- Other seasonal fruits you like
- Cherries

## Preparation

Cut up fruits into chunks or cubes. Place the chunks of fruit onto the wooden skewers. That's all there is to it! You can arrange the fruit randomly or in patterns. Put a fresh cherry (with the pit removed) on the end to look pretty. Have fun!

From: Jenna
To: Mom and Dad
Sent: Monday, September 28, 4:56 PM
Subject: RE: RE: RE: Go, Jenna!

Dad, I like the idea of getting rid of the junk food in the house. PLEASE!! It is really too hard for me to resist it! And I promise, Dad (and Mom!) that I will STOP bringing extra junk into the house and hiding it in my room in my secret stash. That is just NOT helping this situation at all!!

I also really like the idea of keeping busy, doing exercise at the girls gym, eating healthy stuff like those recipes you sent (THANKS for that Dad, and YES let's go shopping together later. It'll be fun!) and just figuring out when I'm eating when I'm NOT even hungry. I think that so much of the time I'm just bored or I don't think of something else to do but eat!!

I'm going to talk to Mrs. Gonzalez later this afternoon. I'll let you know how it goes.

I LOVE YOU GUYS!!

From: Mom and Dad
To: Jenna
Sent: Tuesday, September 29, 7:04 AM
Subject: SO PROUD!!

Jenna, you never cease to amaze us!! Dad and I both agree that if anyone can change, it's you, because you are so intelligent and so strong!

We love you too darling!!!
M & D

Jenna, I'm so glad that you decided to come talk to me today. I had seen you around the halls of our school and always thought you had a great smile. It was wonderful to finally meet you in person!

It took a lot of courage for you to share your feelings with me about your weight and your problems with emotional eating. I feel very special that you decided to share your thoughts and concerns with me. Given that it was our first visit, I was especially impressed by how you realize that you need to change your attitude about yourself and your weight.

Just like we talked about in our meeting, change is not going to happen overnight. You will face some challenges when you work to change your eating habits and to stop your emotional eating. It's not always going to be easy, so I put together an "Action Plan" for you here. It's based on a lot of the things we talked about today. Like we discussed, it will help you be prepared for the challenges that lie ahead. Trying to break the habit of emotional eating is a tough thing to do, even for adults! Read it over and let me know if you have any questions. Looking forward to seeing you soon at our next visit!

See you soon,

Mrs. Gonzalez

# Jenna's Action Plan

## GOAL: Keep Your Attitude Positive!

ACTION
- Think about the present.
- Don't worry about what happened yesterday or a month ago.
- Don't fret about what you're going to do tomorrow or a month from now.
- When you wake up in the morning, tell yourself it's a new day.
- Talk out your feelings when you feel angry, frustrated, or weak.

REMEMBER
- Use positive self-statements — remind yourself of your amazing qualities and talents!

## GOAL: Don't Give Up! Keep at It!

ACTION
- Have realistic goals.
- Don't beat yourself up if you slip up.
- Take baby steps.
- Track your progress with charts or a journal.
- Encourage your support team to cheer you on.

REMEMBER
- Be patient — changes won't happen overnight!

## GOAL: Be Proud and Loud!

ACTION
- Pat yourself on the back.
- Celebrate the small positive changes in yourself.
- Snack on healthy food.
- Tell people close to you about your achievements.
- Work with you parents to create rewards for your milestones.

REMEMBER
- Junk food is not your friend — when you eat junk you're actually punishing your body and mind!

**GOAL: Deal With Your Feelings**

ACTION
- Write in a journal every day.
- Exercise six days a week.
- Relax outside in the park or in the backyard.
- Play your guitar every day.
- Email or call your friends every day.
- Talk out your feelings with friends, family, or a trusted adult.

REMEMBER
- Don't bottle up your feelings — it will only make you want to emotionally eat!

**GOAL: Talk, Talk, Talk**

ACTION
- Email Sara every other day.
- Talk to or email Chris every day.
- Have nightly talk-time with your parents.
- Meet with Mrs. Gonzalez every other week.
- Check in with Mlle. Narby after every French club meeting.

REMEMBER
- Be a good listener — open your ears and your mind to others' ideas and advice!

Jenna's Action Plan

From: Jenna
To: Mrs. Gonzalez
Date: Tuesday, September 29, 5:42 PM
Subject: RE: Action Plan

Mrs. Gonzalez,

Thank you for sending me the Action Plan. I like how you wrote down all the things that we talked about to help me think of ways that I can work on my attitude about myself. I think it will really help me to be nicer to myself, and like you said, to realize that eating too much because I'm feeling bad is not a healthy solution to my problems. Talking to my friends or doing exercise or other fun activities that I like to do is a better idea!

I felt really comfortable with you today and I liked your comfy couch too. Thanks again.

Jenna

From: Mrs. Gonzalez
To: Jenna
Date: Tuesday, September 29, 6:17 PM
Subject: RE: RE: Action Plan

Jenna,

You are most welcome! I noticed that you haven't expressed interest in scheduling another appointment, but I wanted to let you know that if something comes up before then, if you need to talk, please feel free to stop by and let someone in the office know. I'm always here to help students!

Mrs. Gonzalez

OCTOBER

From: Jenna
To: Chris
Date: Friday, October 1, 3:12 PM
Subject: I slipped up…again

Hey dude. Your new song is awesome, in case I forgot to mention that! Just wanted to let you know how things were going. Things are getting better. I talked to the counselor at my school. It helped me more than I thought it would. I didn't realize how many feelings I was keeping inside. It felt good to get them out and to have someone listen to me and give me really good advice.

I've been getting better with my eating but I messed up pretty bad last night. I'm so mad at myself!!! I had a really tough day at school. Some of the kids were looking at me weird, maybe they thought I looked fat in my outfit or something, who knows. Maybe they just need to pick on someone. I don't know. I tried not to let it get to me but it did. I felt bad. And when I got home I fell back into my habit and I feel guilty about it. I ate too many chips and donuts which I found in the kitchen. I have no idea why all that junk food was there! My mom and dad aren't supposed to buy that stuff anymore!!!! ARGH! It really makes me mad that they keep bringing that junk food into the house when they know it's so hard for me to resist it. But there they were – on the counter! Why?!!! But I still shouldn't have eaten them. I knew I was emotional eating, but I felt so bad I really didn't care. How did I slip up so quickly? I told my parents about it and they were really great – they weren't disappointed in me at all and it reminded them again that they need to STOP bringing that type of food home...Anyhow, I'm finally realizing that this IS HARD!!

Your bud,
Jenna

From: Chris
To: Jenna
Date: Friday, October 1, 4:18 PM
Subject: RE: I slipped up...again

Whoa, Jen! Don't be so hard on yourself! Like you said, this is hard! It sounds like you caught yourself before things got really bad again with your eating. And that's awesome! It was really brave for you to tell your parents about your pig-out fest, too.

Look, I'm always here for you when you have bad days. Give me a call and we'll jam or I'll sing to you. Whatever to distract you from your need to feed.

I'm really proud of you for calling yourself out on your emotional eating. That's got to be tough! It sounds like it's even harder to break the habit, but look at how long it took us to get good at guitar playing…it took a lot of time and a lot of calluses on our fingers! Cool that you're talking to your counselor for help. I know some kids at my school (me included) who do that for all sorts of reasons.

Catch ya later Jen!

From: Jenna
To: Chris
Date: Friday, October 1, 7:20 PM
Subject: RE: RE: I slipped up…again

Thanks Chris! It's really good to know that you're always there for me. It's pretty cool that I can realize what makes me run for the closest bag of chips and eat an entire fridge full of food (I've never been THAT bad.). And yeah, talking to the counselor was really great. I really should go back to her I'm going to email her and let her know about what happened, maybe she'll also have some good advice.

See you at practice,
J.

From: Jenna
To: Mrs. Gonzalez
Date: Sunday, October 3, 3:44 PM
Subject: Appointment?

Hi Mrs. Gonzalez,

I hope you had a good weekend. I wanted to set up an appointment with you to talk about something that happened last week. I had a pretty bad slip-up with my eating. It happened after some kids were mean to me, or at least I thought they were. It made me feel really bad, angry, and sad. That night I pigged out on chips and donuts, and the whole time I knew I was doing emotional eating, but right then I didn't care.

I guess the good thing is that I told my parents and friend Chris about what happened, and that helped. My slip-up made me realize again how hard it is trying to change, but I'm still disappointed that I messed up. I've been re-reading the Action Plan that you sent me, especially the part about how each day is a new day…so instead of beating myself up, I'm trying to forgive myself and have decided to start over.

So anyway, I wanted you to know about it and if you have any more great advice for me, that would be cool. I also just want to talk about what I can do to keep from slipping up. Or at least what I can do when it happens. Thanks!

Jenna

From: Mrs. Gonzalez
To: Jenna
Date: Monday, October 4, 8:12 AM
Subject: RE: Appointment?

Jenna,

I am glad that you chose to contact me after your setback. You should be very proud of your honesty in admitting you had a slip-up. You were very smart in making use of the Action Plan. It's always good to remind yourself that each day is a new opportunity to make healthy choices about your eating.

When we met last week, we talked about "emotional triggers," those things that upset you and then make you want to overeat, like when kids are mean. I think what we should spend more time on in our next meeting is figuring out other ways for you to cope with those triggers. By recognizing the things that make you prone to emotional eating and to slip-ups, you will be more prepared to prevent them from happening. Once you know what these things are, you can go to your Action Plan and stop yourself from emotional eating. You could also talk to friends, exercise, play your guitar, or write in a journal to stop your need to eat. That way, you'll have lots of tools to be prepared to deal with slip-ups.

I want to commend you for confiding in your friend Chris and then in me about what happened, instead of keeping the emotional eating episode a secret. I think we both agree that in the past, your keeping the emotional eating a secret only made the problem get more and more out of control. Opening up to people is a huge step, and you should be proud of yourself.

I'm looking forward to seeing you today and talking more about all this!

Mrs. Gonzalez

From: Mom and Dad
To: Jenna
Date: Monday, October 4, 9:23 AM
Subject: Sorry

Sweet Jenna,

Your dad and I wanted to let you know again how proud we are of you. We know how hard it is to change. That's why we wanted to apologize again for bringing the donuts and the chips into the house last week. We were very glad that you told us about your setback and admitted that you had eaten them. We know that was hard for you to do. Like we talked about last night, it wasn't fair for us to bring that junk food into the house. I guess we all may have slip-ups sometimes, including your old faithful Mom and Dad! This is a new learning experience for all of us and if we mess up we just have to pick ourselves up, dust ourselves off, and try harder!

We love you!!

---

From: Jenna
To: Mom and Dad
Date: Monday, October 4, 12:10 PM
Subject: RE: Sorry

---

Hey guys, thanks for admitting that what you did was a mistake, because I was really upset with you about it. Let's all try to do better from now on!

Love ya and see you later. Maybe we'll make the healthy mini-pizzas for dinner tonight!

---

From: Mrs. Gonzalez
To: Jenna
Date: Monday, October 4, 5:21 PM
Subject: Emotional Triggers
Attachment: Jenna's ETs.doc

---

Hi Jenna,

It was a pleasure to see you and to talk to you today. I think you have made some great progress. I'm especially proud of you after today's session because I know how emotional it was for you to talk about some of the painful things on the list you pulled together (see attachment). This is such an important part of your gaining more control over the destructive habit of emotional eating though, even though it's difficult. Just remember to be patient with yourself—things aren't going to be different overnight, but they and you will change. It's already started!

See you at our appointment next week and of course feel free to email me anytime in between or stop by sooner if something else comes up!

Mrs. Gonzalez

---

## My Emotional Triggers*
*by Jenna (with Mrs. Gonzalez)

*Emotional Trigger:* something that makes me want gorge myself by emotional eating

- **Kids are mean to me.** Teasing, bullying, note-passing, or weird looks.
- **Kids exclude me.** Left out because I'm fat. Like in gym class when I'm chosen last for every team.
- **Clothes shopping.** Having to pick out large sizes or shop at plus-size stores.
- **My clothes don't fit right.** Clothes I used to fit into don't fit any more. Or I go shopping for clothes and they don't fit well when I to try them on.
- **Looking in the mirror.** When I look in the mirror and think and see I'm fat.
- **Getting on the scale.** Looking at my actual weight (the stupid number).
- **Being alone.** Feeling lonely because I'm by myself, and I eat to feel like I'm not alone.
- **Boredom.** Feeling bored and not having anything to do, I eat for no reason. Eat away the time…
- **Anxiety.** When I'm worried about something, like my grades or if I messed up.
- **Sadness.** When I'm sad, I go for food to help me feel better, to fill my stomach with something other than sadness.
- **Disappointment.** When I feel disappointed in myself or by other people, like my parents or Angelina Jolie or the world in general.
- **New experiences or situations.** When I have to do something or be somewhere new, I get freaked out and want to eat to calm my nerves.

From: Jenna
To: Mrs. Gonzalez
Sent: Monday, October 4, 8:10 PM
Subject: RE: Emotional Triggers

Mrs. Gonzalez,

Thank you so much for helping me out today. I never realized before how MUCH I used emotional eating to deal with my problems or my bad feelings instead of so many other things I could do! It's a relief to have you to talk to and to have your help figuring all this out. I'm going to show my parents my Emotional Trigger list. (I already showed them my Action Plan.) I've posted them on my bulletin board in my room. I think this is really important stuff and it's going to help me a lot. See you next week!

Jenna

From: Jenna
To: Sara
Sent: Saturday, October 10, 10:19 AM
Subject: UPDATE!
Attachment: Jennasnewbike.jpg

Sarita!! So much has happened since I last wrote to ya! Things are SOOOOOOOO much better, it's not even funny!!

The doc's visit went really well and he gave me all sorts of new ideas about how to get my eating under control. Plus he told me that I don't have any medical problems that are making me "heavy." (Why do adults always use that word?)…My parents have been really helpful too, by doing their best not to bring any more junk food into the house, hooking me up with an awesome yoga class at this new gym for girls, buying me a new bike (which I've been LOVING riding around town – I sent you a pic my mom took of me on it!) and, let's see, what else....Mom and I have been cooking a lot together, much healthier stuff with more veggies... and I've stopped sneaking candy and stuff into my room for late night pig-outs...so all in all, that has been going really awesomely, and I don't get short of breath just from walking up the stairs at school anymore. How proud of me are you?!!!!!

And also, I took your advice and my teacher's advice and I went to talk to my school counselor about my feelings. She has helped me SO MUCH. I'm so glad I decided to talk to her. I've learned to catch myself when I start to think bad thoughts about myself. I realized I was doing that A LOT and it was NOT GOOD!!! It's not easy, and sometimes I still do it, but much less than I used to. I realize now that change is hard, but if I stick to this and keep getting help from my family, my counselor, and my friends I can do it, I know I can!

I'm still playing my guitar too and I've gotten pretty darn good (if I do say so myself!!) I'll have to record a few tunes for ya and send to you by snail mail ;-)

Love ya cuz!!

XOXOX

## About the Author

Lynn R. Schechter, PhD, is a licensed psychologist in private practice. She received her undergraduate degree from Cornell University and her doctoral degree from Columbia University. Dr. Schechter has long been interested in issues related to overweight and obesity in children and has provided therapy and behavioral interventions to many overweight children and their families. She strongly believes that tackling the emotional eating component that contributes to compulsive eating is an essential but often ignored aspect of the complex problem of childhood overweight and obesity.

## About the Illustrator

Jason Chin grew up in New Hampshire, where he was given his first glimpse into the life of an illustrator by his friend and mentor, the acclaimed illustrator Trina Schart Hyman. He attended Syracuse University and, after graduating with a BFA in Illustration, moved to New York City. *Redwoods,* the first book he wrote and illustrated, has received starred reviews and is a Junior Library Guild 2009 selection. Jason has illustrated several other books for children, including *The Day the World Exploded* by Simon Winchester. Jason lives in Brooklyn, New York.